THE ADVENTURE AT LOOKOUT FARM

by

Naida E. Kirkpatrick

Naida E. Kirkpatrick

For the class of Mrs. Schaffer from Emmaus Lutheran School - enjoy Lookout Farm - It was a pleasure to show you the Lincoln Museum

Naida

2-20-07

Royal Fireworks Press

Unionville, New York

Toronto, Ontario

Royal Fireworks Press
First Avenue
Unionville, NY 10988
(914) 726-4444
FAX (914) 726-3824

Royal Fireworks Press
78 Biddeford Avenue
Downsview, Ontario
M3H 1K4 Canada
FAX (415) 633-3010

ISBN: 0-88092-281-8 Paperback
0-88092-282-6 Library Binding

Printed in the United States of America on acid-free, recycled paper using vegetable-based inks by the Royal Fireworks Printing Company of Unionville, New York.

CHAPTER ONE

Going to the Farm

"NO! I won't go! It's a really dumb idea. I don't want to stay at some dumb farm in the middle of nowhere. Why can't I go to Phoenix with you?" Abby stamped her foot and tears burned her eyes. This made her even angrier.

"Baby, don't get so upset." Her mother reached toward her, but Abby jerked away.

"I'm not a baby. Why can't you remember that?"

"I'm sorry." Patricia leaned back in the rocker. "You're right. I forgot again. But you know, Norma Whitaker was my best friend in college. She's asked many times about your visiting them, and this seems like an ideal time since Al and I must be away. Think of it as an adventure. You're always wanting to do something different."

"Oh, sure." Abby plopped down onto the big ottoman. "Some adVENture. Stuck out in the sticks with two kids who probably have to work up to being dumb."

"It might not be as bad as you think," a deep voice spoke from the doorway. "They probably even have hot water and a telephone."

Al Cunningham walked over and sat beside Abby on the ottoman. He gave her long black braid a gentle tug.

"Don't you think you should check them out before you consign them to Dullsville?"

Abby jerked away from him. She jumped to her feet and snapped, "You just want me out of the way, that's what." She stormed down the hall to her room and banged the door behind her. There was a ball of hot wire where her stomach should be. It had been there ever since the afternoon last March when she came home from school and her mother told her that she and Al Cunningham were getting married.

Abby kicked at the wastebasket, spilling most of the contents under the dresser.

"Just think, Abby, we'll be a family again," she mimicked her mother's voice. "Some family. How are we going to be a family when they're sending me to some stupid farm? Besides, I already have a dad. I don't need another one."

Crossing to the window, she shoved it open and stood there taking deep breaths. Abby Randolf was tall for her twelve years. Straight black hair was woven into a thick braid that hung halfway down her back. Her eyes were the color of a winter sky. Now they were full of angry tears, which she kept trying to blink away. The watery, chilly air, smelling of old wet leaves, washed over her. She closed her eyes, remembering the time she and Mom went sledding down the Derby track at the park. What a mistake! The sled hit a chunk of ice, and they went spinning off in different directions. They had laughed all the way home, then had hot chocolate.

"We always had fun, just Mom and me," Abby muttered out loud. "Why does **he** have to come along and spoil everything?"

The following weeks were difficult for everyone. Whenever Al spoke to her, Abby pretended not to hear the first time so Al would have to repeat everything. She spoke to her mother in short, curt sentences, making it clear she was not happy and didn't want anyone else to be either.

The last day of school, Mrs. Shaffer asked everyone in the homeroom to tell what he or she planned to do during vacation. The Murray twins were going to visit their grandparents in Ireland. Ben Justin's sister would be home from college. A few others were visiting relatives. Most were just staying home. Abby was the only one going to a farm. She was **so** embarrassed.

On Saturday Abby and Mom packed Abby's things. That is, Mom packed, and Abby pouted.

"Honey," Mom finally sat down on Abby's bed and patted the space beside her, "sit down. I know you don't want to go to the Whitakers, that you want to come with Al and me. I also know you don't want Al here at all. Wait." She held a finger across Abby's lip as Abby started to speak. "I want more than anything else for the two most important people in my life to be friends. But Abby, a business trip wouldn't be fun for you. I really think you will enjoy the farm if you just give it a fair try." She gave Abby's shoulders a gentle squeeze. "Now, how many shirts will you need?"

The next day was a jumble of church, a scrambled lunch, last minute errands, and then a rush to the train station. Abby felt grown up and scared all at the same time. Al helped her find her seat and stowed her bag on the overhead rack. He watched while she put her ticket in her purse, then he took out a notebook and wrote something on a slip of paper.

"Here." He handed the paper to Abby. "If you need something or get lonesome, you can call us at this number."

He smiled at her. Abby almost smiled back but remembered just in time that she didn't like him. Instead she placed the slip of paper next to her ticket in her purse and turned to wave to her mother standing on the platform.

Abby sat down abruptly as the train jerked into motion. She waved until she could no longer see them on the platform, then leaned back in her seat and looked around at the other passengers. There weren't many. She practically had the whole car to herself. Just then, the door at the end of the car burst open and seven small boys came running through. They romped along the aisle like frisky puppies, followed by a distraught looking young man whose fiery red hair stood up in all directions. There was a green lollipop stuck on his sleeve. He clutched at the seat backs as he struggled after the boys.

Abby smiled at the conductor as he punched her ticket. As she returned it to her purse, the slip of paper Al had given her flipped out. Abby paused. She studied the square block letters and numbers he had written, and she remembered the questioning sound of his voice. For some reason it bothered her that she had snubbed him. She remembered the afternoon not too long ago when she was having so much trouble putting her new seat cover on her bike. Al had found her banging on the seat almost in tears of frustration. Instead of taking over and doing the job for her the way Mom would have done, he just stood in the doorway and gently suggested that she try slipping the cover on from the front first. Pretend it's a glove, he told her. And it had worked.

She had been pretty mean to Al lately. It was really nice of him to tell her how to fix her seat. Maybe he did like her. She slid the paper back into her purse. But, then, why can't I go with them instead of to this dumb farm?

The twisty knot was back in her stomach and Abby felt really alone. Leaning back in her chair, she turned toward the window and stared out at the trees and fields rushing past until darkness hid everything, and Abby could see her reflection and the car behind her in the window.

Abby could feel the drag of the brakes as the train slowed. Awkwardly, she tugged at her bag until she dragged it from the overhead rack. Clutching it and her purse, she moved through the car crabwise, to the door.

Abby hesitated on the platform after the conductor helped her down the steps. Shifting her suitcase to her left hand, she started toward the station. There were only a few people waiting outside, but it was difficult to see because of the bright lights along the edge of the station house.

She felt a touch on her arm as a soft voice said, "You must be Abby Randolf. You look just like Patricia."

Abby turned and looked into the bluest eyes she had ever seen. "Yes, I'm Abby Randolf. Are you Mrs. Whitaker?"

They were out of the bright light now, and Abby could see all of them. Mr. Whitaker: tall and broad shouldered, hair the color of cinnamon; and Mrs. Whitaker: tiny and petite, her hair a swirl of sunshine on top of her head. Beside them stood two Afro-American children. Abby stared in shocked surprise. Mom didn't tell me, was all she could think.

"I'm Marcus. Let me carry that." The tall boy reached for Abby's bag.

"And I'm Molly, and I'm so glad you're here." Both of the children smiled at Abby, their dark skin a sharp contrast to their parents'.

Abby's thoughts chased around her mind like butterflies in a flowerbed. She stood there, bereft of speech, making a few sounds like some idiot and trying to smile. *They probably think I'm a real jerk,* she thought.

As they drove through the darkness, Abby listened to the casual exchange of conversation between the adults. The children were silent. Abby wanted to say something clever just to break the tension that was building, but she couldn't think of anything. It wouldn't *do* to come out with something like, "Hi there. I've never lived with any black people before." She figured they already suspected that. She sat there frozen with embarrassment at her lack of wit.

At last Mr. Whitaker turned the car through a wide gate. At the side of the gate was a large sign with white letters announcing "LOOKOUT FARM PLAYHOUSE."

"Oh, I get it. None of this is real, and we're living in a play." There was a deepening of silence as Abby realized she had actually spoken aloud.

Abby ran up the short ramp to the wide double door. By now, she was tired of being led about. Besides, she had a healthy curiosity, and the old barn looked interesting, to say the least. She saw as she got closer that the tumbledown look of the old barn had been carefully preserved. This made her even more curious.

"Wait! We're not supposed to play around here." Marcus's voice sharpened.

"Why? Are you afraid? Do you suppose it's haunted?" Abby tried to peer through the crack of the double doors. "What do you say we go exploring in here?" She yanked at the latch and managed to pull the doors apart enough for her to slip through. The twins followed, Marcus scolding and protesting as he edged through.

As their eyes slowly adjusted to the dimness, they became aware that they were standing at the back of a theater. Just ahead stretched several rows of chairs arranged in front of a shallow stage. The stage was set like a very old kitchen with pots and dishes scattered about.

"We really shouldn't be in here," Marcus whispered and grabbed Abby's arm. "Let's go."

"Why not? We won't touch anything. It certainly can't hurt to look." Abby shrugged his hand away and walked toward the stage with the twins slowly trailing after her. Once on the stage, she turned to the door leading behind the curtain. As she twisted around, the small rug under her feet slid enough to reveal a short leather strap. At her cry, the twins came running.

"Help me with this," Abby panted as she tugged at the strap. Marcus added his strength, and suddenly a trap door popped open, and the three fell back, scattering like dominos.

"There's a little room down there." Molly's voice sounded hollow and muffled as she leaned over and peered into the opening. With a quick motion she dropped down into the shallow opening, the others following her.

It was a tiny room, crowded with boxes and pieces of furniture and smelling of dust.

"Come on. We have to get out of here." Marcus pulled one of the boxes under the opening and used it as a step to climb through.

It seemed to Abby that they had been in the old barn only a short time, but when they came outside, they discovered the shadows were long, and darkness was beginning to settle.

As they hurried back, Molly asked, "Abby, have you ever been in a play?"

"Oh, once, I think. Marcus, is there another way to get into that room under the stage?"

Marcus shook his head. "How would we know? This is the first time we've been in there, too."

"Well it seems strange to me," Abby persisted. "I mean it didn't look like much, the walls and floor were just dirt. Most basement rooms have a cement floor and walls, don't they? We just have to come back and really explore this barn. Maybe there's a treasure of some kind hidden here. We'll need some light, though. Marcus, do you have a lantern or flashlight we can use?"

"Abby, I told you we're not supposed to be playing here. What makes you think you can just barge in here whenever you like?" Marcus spoke sharply, shaking his head.

Abby could feel her face get hot. How dare Marcus dictate to her! "Is there a ghost? Are you afraid?" she taunted.

"Of course not," Marcus snorted. "We follow rules, that's all."

CHAPTER THREE

Exploring the Hill

Abby sat up suddenly. Blinking her eyes, she slowly focused on the room; the shuttered windows and the books underneath. She slid back under the blanket and tried to straighten out her tangled thoughts. As she lay there she gradually became aware of the silence. Yesterday, Molly had kept up a steady stream of chatter until Abby felt that if she didn't get away she would hold Molly's mouth shut.

"Molly reminds me of those TV ads for the batteries that never quit." She chuckled to herself. "Maybe her batteries have finally stopped." She sat up again and looked toward Molly's bed.

Molly wasn't there. The bed was made up, the blanket folded neatly across the foot. No wonder things were so quiet.

"She's got a lot of nerve going off and leaving me." Abby hurriedly pulled on her clothes. Even though she was tired of Molly's constant chatter, she didn't want to be alone. Snatching up her old blue sweater, she ran downstairs.

Mrs. Whitaker was in the kitchen, cutting up a big pile of vegetables into a tall shiny pot. She turned and smiled at Abby. "You were so tired, we decided to let you sleep." She motioned Abby to the table and took a glass of orange juice and a pitcher of milk from the refrigerator. “The cereal is in that cupboard,” she said, nodding the direction.

When Abby had finished eating and rinsed her dishes, Mrs. Whitaker handed her a bag of bread crumbs.

“Take these out to the chickens, then you and the twins can go exploring. I know they have special things to show you.” She pointed in the direction of the barn and shooed Abby out of the kitchen.

Abby walked slowly toward the barn, the silence ringing in her ears. Turning quickly at a rustling sound behind her, she saw a fat yellow cat pounce on something in the matted grass. To her right stood a huge tree with a wooden bench built around its base. Remnants of last summer’s flowers straggled across a tangled patch. A gentle breeze sighed through the bushy cedars which separated the lawn from the field. The air was cool, with just a hint of warmth mixed in with the tangy whiff of damp earth and old leaves. The knot in her stomach was finally gone, although she was aware only that she felt at ease.

“Well, where do I find these chickens I’m supposed to feed?” Feeling a little miffed, Abby rattled her bag of crumbs. As though a cue were given, there was a sudden onslaught of clucking and chuckling. The chickens had found her! Startled, Abby reached for a handful of crumbs and flung them at the birds. Actually, it was fun. A lot like feeding the pigeons in the park at home.

When the crumbs were all gone, Abby crumpled the bag and stuffed it into her pocket. "That's all there is." She made shooing motions at the chickens. They seemed to understand, gradually wandering off, clucking among themselves.

Abby ambled along too, in the direction of the barn. The closer she got to the barn, the more a pungent, overpowering odor enveloped her. She could hear Molly's voice. "Well," Abby wondered aloud, "I guess the batteries haven't run down, after all. Doesn't she *ever* stop talking?"

She finally found the twins. Each had on a long dark canvas apron and tall black boots. They were cleaning Old Charger's stall. Marcus had just finished filling a wheelbarrow with a mixture of straw and dung. Molly was forking clean straw from a large bale and spreading it about over the floor of the stall.

"Is that a pitchfork you're using?" Abby pointed to the tool Molly was handling so expertly.

"Yep." Molly continued to spear fresh straw from the bale.

"Ugh." Abby held her nose while she watched. "How often do you do this?"

"Every week." Marcus put away the shovel and taking hold of the wheelbarrow handles, trundled the load outside where he dumped the straw mixture into a pile beside the barn. He then rinsed out the wheelbarrow and leaned it against the wall.

Abby gave a shudder of distaste. The air made her eyes sting, and she was afraid that if she took a deep breath, her breakfast would come up.

Molly pulled off her gloves and apron. “There! That’s done. Let’s go explore the hill. We have something to show you, Abby.”

The three explorers left the barn and followed a path along a row of scrubby bushes. Gradually, the ground began to rise, and the path ended as they began climbing. The trees on the hill were just beginning to show tiny, pale green leaves. At their feet were patches of fragile spring flowers.

They climbed steadily for nearly an hour. Some places were bare dirt, which packed firmly under their feet. Occasionally, a small outcropping of rock provided a step of sorts for them to scramble up. By using the rocks and tufts of grass as stepping stones, they finally reached a level area. It was a small space, but at least it was flat. Across one side lay a chunk of an old tree trunk. Marcus stopped, then sagged down onto the log.

“Let’s rest, OK?” He pulled his shirt sleeve across his forehead. Molly and Abby dropped onto the soft grass and stretched their legs straight out in front of them. As they sat there, each panting from the climb, Abby realized how intensely quiet it was. Even Molly was silent. The only sounds were an occasional bird call in the distance and the hiss of the wind through the branches of the trees.

"Well, Abby, how do you like our view? This is what we wanted to show you." Marcus made a sweeping gesture which took in the whole countryside.

"It's beautiful." Abby leaned back on her elbows. She felt relaxed and almost happy. For the moment, she had forgotten to be angry.

Spread out below them lay the whole farm like a giant mural with many shades of green interrupted here and there with splashes of brown. Along the left ran a fence row of tangled black bushes. Across one corner, a tiny stream twisted along. Over to the right was the farmhouse. Just below them stood a windmill behind an old tumble-down barn.

"Look." Abby pointed to the old barn. "Is that the barn we went in yesterday? From here it looks like it's ready to fall down."

"Yep, that's the one." Marcus studied the ground as he spoke. "I guess it's been there for about two hundred years. It's not used any more. Not for farming anyway. It's really a playhouse now. The Community Players use it for a theater. That's why it's got a stage and all that other stuff.

"Oh look!" He leaped to his feet and began clawing at the dirt beside the old log.

"Marcus! What in the world—" Abby sat up and clutched Molly's arm.

"Just look at this!" Marcus held out a piece of stone.

"How nice. A rock. You make all this commotion over just a stone?" Abby's sarcasm displayed her annoyance.

"No, no." Marcus's eyes glistened with excitement. "Not just a stone, an arrowhead. See?" He carefully rubbed the mud away and polished the stone on his sleeve until Abby could see the ridges and planed surfaces of the triangular stone.

"The Miami Indians used to live in this part of the country. They probably hunted in this very spot. I can add this to my collection." He turned to Abby, "Would you like to see my collection?"

"Sure." Abby sat back down beside Molly. "But why don't you tell me more about the old barn?"

Marcus and Molly exchanged a look. "There isn't much to tell." Molly pulled at the grass as she talked. "It's just an old barn that is used sometimes by the theater folks, and we're not supposed to play around there."

"Yeah, Abby." Marcus, suddenly serious, sat up very straight. "Never go into the old barn alone."

Once Abby's curiosity was tickled, she just had to know more. "Why? I plan to explore it some more. Wouldn't you like to come with me? You never did tell me whether it's haunted."

Much to her annoyance, the twins exploded with laughter.

"You bet." Marcus held his sides. "It's haunted by the Saturday Spook."

"Oh really! You act like you know everything. There aren't such things as spooks." Abby sniffed and jumped to her feet. She was tired of this game. "Let's go."

She started off along a path leading away from their resting place. The twins scrambled along behind her.

"A long time ago," Marcus explained as he caught up with her, "this path was part of a wagon trail around the hill." He described so vividly how the wagons were driven in a spiral fashion that Abby could almost see the horses straining and pawing at the soft dirt of the trail.

"How do you know all this stuff?" Abby sounded annoyed. She felt as though she was in school.

"I read about it. I just like to know what happened long ago and why things are the way they are." Marcus fell silent.

Abruptly the path ended at a wall of tumbled rock, scrubby trees and tangled vines. As they retraced their steps, Molly gave Abby a sidelong glance. "Would you like to be in our play, Abby?"

"What play is this?"

"It's called 'Dangerous Journey,' and it will be given the first Saturday night next month, and I think it would be fun if we could all be in it. Mama could speak to

Mrs. Ambrose and find a part for you. What do you think?"

"No thanks. You don't have to fit me in. I don't need anyone feeling sorry for me."

"No one is feeling sorry for you. I just thought it would be fun if we all were in the play together." Molly's reply was stiff, and for once her cheerfulness was gone.

"I told you she wouldn't be interested, Molly." Marcus' words were flat and restrained.

With a swish of her pony tail, Abby shrugged past Molly and started down the hill.

It was much easier going down, and she soon put some distance between them. *What a fool I am!* she thought angrily. *We were having such fun, and I thought they liked me. But they're just feeling sorry for me.*

"Come on, Abby, don't get mad," Molly called after her.

"Yeah, Abby, don't be crabby. Crabby Abby, crabby Abby." Marcus chimed in with a chuckle at his rhyme.

Abby could hear them laughing at their joke. She walked faster to get away from the sound. It was difficult to maintain her dignity with her feet sliding under her. She skittered and slid on the damp grass and loose rock.

"Abby! Wait!" The twins called to her, but she just ran faster. All at once, she stumbled and lost her balance completely. Rolling over and over, bumping elbows and knees, she finally came to an abrupt halt. She lay there panting, looking up through the branches of what appeared to be an immense bush.

"Ouch!" She struggled to free herself from the prickly branches. Her jeans were torn at the knees, and her right elbow burned.

"I tried to warn you." Molly peered at her and brushed Abby's hair away from her face.

"Abby! Are you OK?" Marcus held out a hand to help her up.

"I'm fine." She ignored his outstretched hand and with much effort elbowed her way out of the grasp of the bush. Her knees burned, and her right arm was beginning to throb.

Molly giggled. "You looked kind of funny rolling down into that bush. I'm glad you're not hurt, but you sure look a mess."

"I'm so glad you're amused." Abby's eyes sparkled with angry tears. With that, she whipped around and marched off, trying to keep from limping.

The rest of the afternoon was strained since Abby refused to talk to anyone. Supper came and went, and Abby finally went to bed, feeling completely alone and desolate.

After breakfast the next morning, Molly, as cheerful as ever, continued the discussion about the play.

"I really think you'd like to be in our play, Abby. We really—"

"What is so special about this play you've been nagging me about?" Abby slammed the magazine she had been looking at down onto the table. "You've been babbling on about your stupid play ever since I got here."

"It's not a stupid play, it's historical. You're the one who's stupid." Molly's eyes flashed with anger as she glared at Abby.

"What part do you have in mind for me? A famous clown so you can have something else to laugh about?" Abby stood as tall as she could, her arms clutched across her chest. She was so angry her stomach felt as if she had swallowed a ball of hot lead. She spit out her words with fury. "I don't need anyone feeling sorry for me. I can take care of myself just fine, thank you. Besides, I just plain don't want to be in your dumb play!"

"What's the matter, Whitey? Think you're too good for us? I don't know why I should feel sorry for you. You do a fine job of it all by yourself." Molly's eyes flashed with anger as she glared at Abby. She stood firmly with feet spread apart, hands on her hips. Her head jutted forward, giving her the appearance of a feisty, snarling puppy. "I thought you might like to meet some of our friends, but I don't think I want them to meet you now."

"Who do you think you are, calling me names? Besides, if your *friends* all chatter as much as you do, I don't think I want to meet them." Abby's face was pale, and her eyes resembled slivers of ice.

"What's that supposed to mean?"

"It means why don't you shut up once in a while. Did you ever stop to think that some people don't want to be chattered at all the time? Maybe someone else would like to talk once in a while."

With that parting shot, she stamped out of the room and stormed up the stairs. Snatching her sweater from the chair, she rushed back down the stairs and out of the house. She wanted to run as far as she could to get away from the hurt and anger that overpowered her.

CHAPTER FOUR

New Friends

The next few days were difficult for everyone. Abby and Molly were extremely polite while Marcus answered Abby's questions with an abrupt "yes" or "don't know." Loneliness clutched at her until she ached. It seemed that everything she did was wrong. However, life doesn't stand still on a farm, and chores still had to be done.

One morning after breakfast, Abby stacked the dishes and, turning to Mrs. Whitaker, said, "I'll wash these up while you finish your coffee."

"Wouldn't you rather help the twins, Abby?" Mrs. Whitaker asked as she sipped her coffee.

"No, I'd rather do this."

"Abby, do you feel uncomfortable around the twins? They do take a little getting used to."

"What do you mean?" Abby stalled.

"I think you know what I mean," Mrs. Whitaker smiled at Abby.

Abby hesitated. "I don't know. Maybe a little. I just feel all mixed up about a lot of things." If only she could tell someone how hurt and angry and scared she felt, but she didn't know how to go about it. Instead Abby shrugged. "Nothing's really wrong. I was just afraid they would ask me to help clean the barn, and I don't think I can handle that. Besides," Abby hesitated, then blurted out, "Molly called me 'Whitey.' No one has ever called me names like that."

"Oh dear." Mrs. Whitaker frowned. "That's rough. That old saying about sticks and stones just isn't true. I know how you feel. Names can really hurt. We knew when we adopted the twins, it would present problems for all of us. It's not a common thing for a couple like us to adopt a black child, let alone two. But when the church told us about them, we just couldn't turn away. They had no family at all, and we just couldn't separate them. For the most part, they have learned to handle the looks and comments pretty well, but it isn't easy for them."

Molly couldn't stay angry for long, and gradually, the ice between the two girls began to melt. She showed Abby how to hang the laundry on the clothesline, whooping with laughter at Abby's clumsy attempts to stretch a sheet on the line while the wind whipped it about. Finally, after chasing ne of the cats that ran off with a sock, the two girls sat on the tree bench panting and laughing.

"Molly," Abby became serious. "I'm really sorry I was so mean to you. I shouldn't have said all that stuff."

Molly nudged her shoulder against the other girl. "Don't feel bad. You only said what Marcus has been telling me for as long as I can remember."

Abby was quiet for a while, then in a rush of words, blurted, "Molly, do you mind that Jake isn't your real father?" Abby's stomach knotted up. The answer was so important.

"What? " Molly looked surprised. "You mean because I'm adopted?"

"Yeah. That and the fact that you're black and he's not."

Molly was silent. Abby felt miserable. There! She had goofed again.

Molly spoke slowly, as though she were choosing her words as she went. "Being adopted doesn't really bother me. Doesn't bother Marcus, either. We talk about it a lot. Things like Mama being so careful about not getting sunburned, and the way she has to curl her hair. You see, we've always been here. We were only babies when we were adopted, so we don't remember anywhere else. Mama told us that our real mother died during a terrible storm, and they don't know anything about our real father."

"Oh, Molly. That's tough." Abby didn't know what to say. At least she knew who her father was, even though he wasn't around much.

"You want to know what really bugs me, Abby?" Molly's voice sharpened. "It's those do-gooders at church who come up and pat me on the head and say dumb things to Mama like, 'Isn't she sweet?,' and, 'They're so adorable.' 'You're doing such a noble thing, Norma.' Just like we're pets or something."

Abby shrugged. "Grown-ups always say dumb things."

Molly snorted. "It's not just grown-ups. Ask Marcus how he likes to be treated like part of the wall. We didn't have any real problems until last year."

"What happened last year?"

"It was after school began. A new kid moved here from Richmond and began to hassle Marcus. Our school isn't very large, so everyone is in each class with everyone else. Anyway, every time Marcus would say something in class or ask a question, Arthur, that's his name, would make quacking noises. Then he got to calling him names, told him we should go back to Africa and all sorts of stuff. Actually we didn't come from Africa. We're just as much American as anyone else." Molly jumped up and paced back and forth. "One day he said some really nasty stuff about Mama and me, and Marcus just about took Arthur apart. If it hadn't been for some of the other guys in the hall, I don't know what would have happened. Anyway, Papa and Arthur's dad and Mrs. Werther, the principal, had a very long conference."

"That's terrible. What happened after that?"

"Well," Molly sat down on the bench. "Arthur keeps his distance. He has some friends, and they still make remarks, but we pretty much keep out of each others' way. Mrs. Werther said that we all have to learn to get along."

Abby was silent for so long that Molly finally asked, "You OK?"

Abby shook her head slowly. "I guess I just never thought about how you must feel. Some people are so dumb. You're always so happy and all, I just never supposed you had problems. Besides, why did you call me 'Whitey'?"

"Girl, now *you're* being dumb." Molly jumped up from the bench and faced Abby. Placing her hands on her hips, she studied the other girl intently, then announced, "You just have to come with us next week to the Murray's party. Then you'll see what I'm talking about."

"Why?"

"Just wait. You'll see. Meanwhile, think about the play."

"Argh! I'll tell you something, Molly, but you mustn't tell Marcus. Promise?" At Molly's nod, Abby continued. "I told you I thought your play was dumb. Actually, I just cannot stand up in front of people. I was in a play once, and my tights split, and everyone laughed, and I just wished I could *die*." Abby shuddered.

Molly gave her a sidelong glance. "Well, maybe we could find a part where you wouldn't need to wear tights."

"Get out of here." Abby gave her a playful shove. "Don't you ever give up?"

"Nope. I'm cheerful *and* stubborn." Grabbing up the empty basket, she darted away. "Race you back!"

The days began to blur together, much like crayons melting. Days of sunshine and sharp winds. Abby learned to drive the big tractor, sitting up on the tall seat, feeling the thunder of power throbbing through the huge machine. She found out exactly what Marcus meant by planting the garden. Her back ached for two days, and she was convinced her knees would never be straight again.

"All this for just vegetables. Why don't you just go to the store and buy them?" she burst out finally, at the end of her endurance.

Marcus paused, and shoving his cap back, flashed a superior smile. "Where do you suppose the store gets its vegetables, huh?"

Abby fled to the woods every chance she got. The whispering of the trees calmed her angry feelings, and it helped to stamp around in the leaves. Sometimes she felt as though she was mad at everyone. Mom doesn't want me around now that she has Al; the Whitakers are nice to me, but they're not family. And Molly! How can she possibly be that cheerful. It must be an act.

One particularly trying day, Molly had brought up the subject of the play again, and Abby had rushed out to the woods. She stamped through the paths, causing the mud to splash up around her ankles. "I wish everyone would just leave me alone for once. I'd like to decide for myself what I want to do. I told her I don't want to be in that play. Why does she keep asking about it?"

As she kicked at a stump, she lost her balance and landed flat on her back in a pile of leaves and underbrush. "Ooph." As she lay there staring at the branches far above her, she felt something beneath her give way, and she dropped into a slot in the ground. Abby sat up and looked about her. She seemed to be in a small chamber, but there were so many leaves that it was hard to tell.

"I have to tell Molly about this." Abby pulled herself out of the hole and took off for the house at a dead run. "Molly, you'll never guess what I just found!" Abby's announcement was interrupted by Mrs. Whitaker calling to them from the other room.

"Come meet our new choir director!"

Abby followed Molly into the study, trying to straighten her shirt as she went.

Mr. Whitaker and a strange woman with red hair were having a discussion. A lively one it appeared, considering the amount of hand waving on the part of the stranger. Marcus was showing his collection of arrowheads to a young man.

"Oh! It's you," Abby gasped in surprise. The others stared at her. The stranger's bright blue eyes twinkled at her from below his frazzled red hair.

CHAPTER FIVE

Underground Railroad

"Of course it's me. Who else would I be?" he laughed. "I'm Rob. Who are you?"

Abby was achingly aware of her muddy jeans and tangled hair. Awkwardly, she sat down on the stack of fat cushions by the window.

"I mean from the train. You were on the train I came here on. I mean, I saw you with a bunch of little boys."

"Ah! The angelic ones." He laughed, and his eyes crinkled up into slits. "Come." He motioned to her. "Have you seen these?"

"These," were Marcus's collection of arrowheads, seven stone points, all arranged carefully on a bed of cotton. Abby examined the stones, then carefully picked one up. "Why is this one different? It seems longer and thinner."

"That's a spear point." Marcus pointed to a series of grooves around the base of the stone. "Here is where a thong was wrapped around to hold it onto a spear." The rest of his explanation was cut short by the loud voices across the room.

"But we don't have anyone else, Jake." The red-haired woman paced back and forth, still waving her arms.

"My mother is all wrapped up in this play," Rob shrugged. "She even has my choir involved. She never lets up." He turned back to Marcus and the arrowheads.

"What do you mean, 'Your choir'?" Abby persisted.

"I am at the Academy, and we have just returned from a tour. My name is Rob Ambrose. My mother is directing 'Dangerous Journey.' If you don't have a part yet, watch out. Mother will be gunning for you." With another brilliant smile, he turned once more to Marcus and the arrowheads.

"Not you too!" Abby groaned. "I'm fed up with hearing about this play."

"Do you know anything about it?" Rob paused to eat a cookie, then continued. "About a hundred and fifty years ago, this farm was part of a system known as the Underground Railroad. That's where it got its name of Lookout Farm. The people living here were just poor farmers, but the idea of slavery was so abhorrent to them that they felt they should do what they could to help stop it. Runaway slaves were helped from one safe place to another until they reached someplace in the North where they could live as free people. Some even went as far as Canada."

"So? What's the big deal?"

"Well, the *big deal* was, that if they were caught, *everyone* suffered. The slave was sent back to his master, and those who helped them were punished, even to the point of losing everything they owned." He leaned closer and in a low voice said, “I’ve heard there is a hidden room somewhere under the barn where the runaways were kept until it was safe for them to continue their journey.” He looked behind him, then in a whisper added, “There is even a special treasure hidden there.”

A serious Abby turned to Molly. “We need to talk. I just found something that needs to be checked out.”

CHAPTER SIX

The Tunnel

As soon as the chores were out of the way the next morning, Molly and Abby started off toward the woods.

"Let's check this out first, then we'll tell Marcus about it," Abby suggested. " Marcus always lectures so."

Quickly she found the place where she had fallen the day before, and the two girls carefully lowered themselves into the opening. Abby pulled a couple of flashlights from her jacket pocket. Handing one to Molly, she began to shine her light around.

It was a shallow chamber, long and narrow, and the girls carefully stepped across the soft earth floor.

"Look!" Molly motioned with her light. "This looks like a tunnel of some kind."

"Let's see where it goes." Abby led. The tunnel was surprisingly dry after the entrance. The walls were cool to the touch, the ceiling almost dusty. It wasn't very high, and Abby had to stoop a little.

"Do you suppose this is part of the railroad system?" Molly's voice sounded curiously flat.

As they walked, they became aware that the floor was gradually dropping, and after a while, they could stand upright with plenty of headroom.

"Molly, come here." Abby motioned Molly over to a panel set on the dirt wall. "Is this what I think it is?"

"It looks like a door. Let's get it open." But even after much tugging and pounding, the door would not budge. Abby leaned against the wall to rest. "We'll have to get some help. This is stuck too hard. Let's come back in a day or two."

Much to their frustration, the bright, sparkling days came to an abrupt end, as they often do in the Midwest. The skies turned as dull as pewter, and it rained steadily. The girls could not explore the tunnel under such conditions.

"Molly, we have to do something or I am going to go nuts! Come on." Grabbing Molly by the arm, Abby hunted up Mrs. Whitaker. "We need to go to the library. Will you take us?"

It took much digging but they finally found what they were seeking. "Molly, listen to this." Abby read from a book she had discovered. "A slave named Caleb Walker and his granddaughter Sukey, arrived at the Lookout Farm on the evening of January 15. It was dark and very cold. As they stood in the open doorway with lamplight flickering on their weary faces, the sounds of horses and barking dogs echoed through the snowy woods. Quickly they were hurried inside and taken to a place of safety. Their only possessions were a shabby green carpetbag and a small doll made of cornhusks which Sukey clutched." Abby stopped.

"Well, is that all? Nothing more about them?" Molly was impatient.

"Just a little more about how they were never seen again. I guess they must have got away. But still," Abby stared at Molly. "Rob said there is supposed to be a hidden room somewhere under the barn where the runaways stayed until it was safe to travel. Do you suppose it's connected to that tunnel we found?"

"Sure." Molly's dimples flashed. "And when we get the door open, we'll probably find their bones."

It was almost a week before the skies cleared enough for the explorers to continue their search. By now, the two conspirators had included Marcus. He listened thoughtfully as Abby described the tunnel in the woods, sketching a map as she talked.

"It sounds like we will need some tools to open that door." He thought a while, then jumped to his feet. "I'll get some tools and meet you in half an hour. You get some lights, extra batteries and something to eat."

Molly ran off to gather up their flashlights and batteries. Abby scurried about the kitchen, opening cupboards and slamming doors. She quickly slapped together a few sandwiches which she stuffed, along with three apples, into her backpack.

The tunnel was still dry despite all the rain. The three carefully searched the small entryway, then started down the long tunnel. Abby led the way, followed by Molly.

Marcus brought up the rear, trying to measure and draw a map as they went.

"Can you just imagine what it must have felt like to creep through here when it was cold and dark and you could hear dogs chasing you?" Molly's voice sounded as though her words were drawn through a filter.

"It must have been pretty scary." Abby shook her head, brushing at the cobwebs which drooped across their path. It was slow traveling, having to pick their way with only the flashlights for guidance. Besides, Marcus was trying to measure as well. Abby became impatient.

"Why don't I go on ahead and find the door, then you can follow my light?" She didn't wait for an answer, but strode on ahead and promptly stumbled over something.

"How about that! The floor just tripped me," she tried to joke as she rubbed her knees. As the twins came running up, she pointed her light at the spot where she fell. "Be careful. We don't want any more accidents."

When they reached the panel in the wall, Marcus put away his sketches and tapes. Taking a crowbar from his bag, he attacked the door. Molly and Abby each took a tool and began chipping away at the dirt which was packed around the edges.

"Wow! This is as hard as cement. Do you suppose it wasn't meant to be opened?" Abby paused to catch her breath. "We may get this off and find only a wall of dirt, after all."

Marcus stopped, and rapped several times on the panel. "It sounds pretty empty to me. I think there's a room on the other side."

Molly made a face and clutched her hands up around her head. "OOOH, what if something knocks back at us?" She giggled.

Abby sniffed. "Don't be silly. Get back to work." They all resumed chipping and banging. Slowly the door was freed from its seal of rock-hard mud. As they pushed, it gave suddenly, and all three tumbled inside as the door crashed against the wall.

"Quick. Get the lights." Abby, coughing and sneezing, struggled to breathe in the swirling dust. As the dust settled, they carefully shined their lights all around. They were in a small room that had been carved out of the earth. Each wall was supported by wooden planks, which slanted diagonally and met at the corners. The bracing was crude and uneven, just like the wall. In one corner stood a rickety little table and a chair with one broken leg.

"Do you suppose this is where Caleb Walker waited, Molly?" Abby prowled around the room. "Rob also said there was hidden treasure here. Do you suppose it could be Sukey's doll?"

"What doll? And who's Caleb Walker? What has he to do with any of this?" Marcus spoke sharply, although his voice was as muffled as the others.

“Let’s take a break. Here.” Abby handed each twin a sandwich and unwrapped one for herself.

“Caleb Walker was a runaway slave who came through Lookout Farm with his granddaughter. She had a cornhusk doll. We think he may have been hidden here.” Molly explained through a mouthful of bread and cheese.

“Well, there’s nothing here but dust. We might as well go back.” Finishing his lunch, Marcus brushed his jacket and packed the tools away in his bag. The girls reluctantly followed him after carefully pulling the door shut behind them.

“I wonder what kind of treasure could be hidden here. It’s not a very big room.” Abby sounded as though she were thinking out loud.

“Maybe there were jewels hidden in the doll.” Molly sneezed. “Whatever it was, it probably has turned to dust by now.”

After they climbed out of the tunnel and were stuffing all their gear away, Marcus turned to Abby. “You know, there might be another possibility. Maybe this treasure was a paper of some kind.”

“What kind of paper? A letter?”

“Yeah. We studied this in school. I don’t know, maybe a certificate of freedom or something.” Marcus slung his bag across his shoulder and started off through the trees. Abby stared after him. He had just given her a marvelous idea.

CHAPTER SEVEN

Abby's Accident

The days seemed to be rushing by, and even though Abby thought constantly about the Underground Railroad, she still managed to become involved with other things. Without realizing it, she and the twins were becoming good friends and had relaxed enough so that Abby and Molly would argue over almost anything while Marcus played the amused referee. It was great fun.

One brisk, sparkling morning, Rob showed up with an extra bicycle which he elaborately explained was his sister's, but Abby could use it while she visited. The four of them took off down the road in a swirl of dust.

Abby felt as though she was flying as she raced along, hair streaming behind her, shoulders hunched over handlebars, knees pumping.

"Race you to that clump of trees!" she yelled as she flashed past the twins.

With a flash of spokes and much puffing the three skidded to a stop at a fence bordering a line of tall bushes. As they waited for Rob to catch up they leaned on their bikes, panting. When Rob finally braked to a stop, Molly and Abby were deep in another argument.

"I didn't say you're a weird family. You're just making that up, Molly." Abby's smile tightened beneath her cold eyes.

"Well, you said you thought it odd that we're so different. That's the same as weird."

"Hey! What's going on? I thought you were all such good friends, and here you are, throwing darts." Rob leaned his bike against the fence and dropped onto the grass. "It's too nice today to fuss, so why don't you two stop arguing?"

"Oh, Abby's just jealous because we have such fun as a family."

"Am not! You think you're so smart." Abby turned and looked back at the road they had just traveled.

Marcus pulled Molly aside, and the two walked slowly away, along the fence, Marcus poking at the ground with a long stick. Rob leaned against a post, as Abby stood, still gazing off across the field.

"You want to talk about it?" His voice was as bland as pudding.

"About what?"

"I don't know. Whatever is *really* bothering you."

"Nothing's bothering me. I'm just fine." Abby jerked her bike into position and jumping on, pedaled off across the field. "I wish everybody would just leave me alone," she screamed the words into the wind as she bounced across the uneven meadow. It was exciting to push against the wind, making it give way for her. Abby laughed and yelled, her anger slowly dissipating. She made a wide slow turn and headed back toward the blur that was Rob by the fence. As she stood on the pedals to jump a small ridge, a large bird rose suddenly from the tall grass and flew in front of her.

"Look out, bird," Abby, caught off guard, jerked her handlebars and twisted in order to avoid the creature. With a crash, she landed on her side with her right leg caught under the bike. "You stupid bird! I'd like to chop you into little pieces. Look what you've done!" Abby pulled and tugged, but her pants leg was caught in the chain, and she couldn't reach it to free herself.

When the others finally reached her, Marcus surveyed Abby with a gleam of annoyance in his eyes. "Seems like I'm always having to untangle you from something." After freeing her jeans, he righted the bike and checked it over. "Everything seems to be working OK. You can ride it back." He pushed it over to Abby, then rode away.

"That was a pretty good stunt, Abby," Molly's eyes twinkled. "Do you think you could do it again when we get home so Mama and Papa can see?" She chuckled at her own joke.

"You know, Molly, you're always laughing at me, and I'm sick of it." Abby rode away, being very careful to avoid rough spots.

As Rob and Abby followed the twins home, Abby suddenly burst out, "I hate it here, and I hate these people. I wish I could go home this very minute." She looked over at Rob. "I shouldn't have said that. I didn't mean you." She had that elevator feeling in her middle that indicated she had said too much.

"I thought you were having a good time Abby. Hate is a pretty strong word, you know."

"Oh, they're OK, I guess. Maybe I don't really *hate* everyone. They just seem too good to be true sometimes."

"How? I'm not sure I know what you mean." Rob sounded puzzled.

"Oh, like Marcus always helps with the chores without grumbling. Molly's so cheerful it makes me sick, and the Whitakers always seem to have time to sit and listen. My mom is always working or busy or something. And now she has Al."

"Well, sometimes things aren't always just the way they seem," Rob slowed to let Abby ride along the drive ahead of him. "At least, it's something to think about."

That evening Abby went to bed early. "My leg is a little sore, I must have pulled something," she told Mrs. Whitaker. Actually, she wanted to be by herself for a while. She had some thinking to do. Mrs. Whitaker had said once that things were difficult for the twins. Maybe they aren't always such a happy family. Abby and her mother usually got along quite well, but there were times when they rubbed each other the wrong way. Abby wasn't a person who spent much time speculating. "I must have a serious talk with Molly," she decided. She propped her aching leg on a pillow and fell asleep.

CHAPTER EIGHT

Meeting Old Charger

The days settled back into their usual pattern of chores before fun. Abby realized with surprise that she looked forward to the time in the garden. "I never thought making a garden could be fun," she told Mr. Whitaker. He had paused on his way to the barn.

"Abby, you sound like a true farmer," Mr. Whitaker smiled.

"Can I tell you something? Promise you won't tell the twins?" At his nod, she continued. "I have names for some of my plants. This is the Pepper family, Paula, Patty and Trixie. Here are Zelda and Zack Zucchini. And over there is Barney and Barbara Beanrow."

"You have a very unique garden." Mr. Whitaker pointed to the other rows. "What about the carrots and the other things? Do they have names, too?"

"Oh no. I don't name things I can't see." And she returned to hoeing carefully around the bean plants.

That evening right in the middle of dinner, Mom called.

"Honey, I think we may be finishing our business here a little sooner that we expected. Are you having a good time?"

"Sure." Abby almost told her about the tunnel but stopped quickly. Better to save that until they really found something. "Mom, why didn't you tell me that the twins are Afro-American?"

"I thought it would be better if you didn't make up your mind in advance. How are things going?" Mom sounded concerned.

"We went to this party at the home of some people named Murray. It was really neat. They have a boy who is Afro-American, too. There were other people there who have adopted mixed kids. Every month they get together and have a party or cookout and talk about things like how to handle the dumb things other people say to them. The kids even have their own discussion, too."

"What did you talk about?" Mom sounded curious.

"I mostly listened. They talked about school and TV and different ways to braid hair. Did you know it takes almost three hours for Molly to fix her hair in those tiny braids?"

"Are there many children in your group?"

Abby was silent as she pictured the group in the family room at the Murray's. "Maybe about ten or so. One girl couldn't come because she was away at college, and there was another family whose kids were sick with chickenpox."

"Are there many your own age?"

"Well, there are Molly and Marcus, of course. Then Andrea who is American and Korean, Jason who is Afro-Japanese, and Morgan who is Afro-American. The rest are little kids."

When their conversation was over, Abby went back to finish her dinner. As she ate, she reflected on the party at the Murray's. It really had been fun, much to her surprise. She had beaten Morgan at checkers several times, but the best part was listening to them talk about things that "they" said or did. When she finally realized that "they" were people like herself, Abby felt really uncomfortable. Then suddenly, Andrea looked up at Abby and said with a smile, "Abby, you realize we're not talking about *you*. Just the fact that you're here makes you different."

As the time for the performance of "Dangerous Journey" grew closer, the twins were often busy with additional rehearsals. At last Abby had all the time she wanted alone. One afternoon everyone had gone into town, and Abby had the whole farm to herself. It was the perfect opportunity to explore the old barn without having Marcus scold or try to scare her by jumping from behind things. She collected what she called her exploring gear, her flashlight and an old putty knife, and cautiously slid through the big double door of the barn.

The silence hurt her ears. As she waited for her eyes to adjust to the dim light, she heard little scrabbling sounds, and soft whispers.

Ahead was the stage where they had found the trapdoor. To the left were stacks of chairs. Against the wall behind the chairs were stacks of baskets and some old, dusty parts of farm equipment. On her right was a series of steps, really not much more than a fancy ladder leading to a narrow balcony. This ran along one wall and ended in a large room with two sides.

"Well, let's see where this goes," Abby spoke aloud, her words echoing dully in the silence. Carefully, she clambered up the ladder. The balcony was no more than a ledge just wide enough to walk, one foot ahead of the other. The room at the end was filled with hay. Abby took a deep breath and immediately sneezed. Once, twice, three times. A window as big as a door dominated the far side. Abby went over to it, stepping clumsily over the slippery hay. The view made her gasp with surprise. She could see the woods almost at tree-top level. "Wow! This is where they got the name of Lookout Farm. You could see someone coming from way off."

She turned and bounced back across the springy hay to the ledge, but she underestimated her distance and felt herself sliding. Grabbing wildly, still clutching her light, she fell in a slide of hay to land flat on the tiny stage. She picked herself up and brushed away the dust and bits of hay. "Now that I've seen the upstairs, I'll have a look at the downstairs." Abby pulled open the trap door and slid through the opening. The room looked the same as before, dusty and small. Slowly, Abby focused her light in a path around the area. The darkness looked different somehow along a short wall, just behind a stack of barrels. Abby's curiosity prodded her into activity. She shoved and tugged at the barrels until they scooted away from the wall far enough to expose a large picture.

"This is so dirty, I can't even see what it's about." She started to brush away some of the dust and cobwebs when the picture toppled to the side, revealing an opening. "Well! Now we're getting somewhere. Maybe this leads to the hidden room." Cautiously, Abby stepped into the opening, shining her light all around. It was just a roughly scooped out passageway, narrow and cramped. Although the walls were dry and firm, the air felt cool and after a few minutes, Abby began to shiver. The floor was rough and uneven, so her progress was snail-like.

It seemed like she had been creeping along forever when she realized she was now climbing. The walls were still dry, but underfoot the earth became softer and more difficult to manage. Abby concentrated on maintaining her balance and was caught by surprise when the tunnel ended abruptly.

"Huh? Now what? Did I come all this way just to go back?" She flashed her light around, but there was nothing but dirt and the tunnel behind her. "This is just great. If this were TV, there would be a panel in the wall or a trapdoor or *something*." She stood on one foot and then the other while she drew circular patterns on the walls with her light. "Well," she reasoned aloud, "I have been going uphill for a while. Maybe at one time this led outside somewhere." She jabbed at the ceiling with her hands and felt something give ever so slightly. As she pounded with all her strength, Abby felt something give way completely, and she exploded from her space like a cork from a bottle.

"Oh NO!" Abby was shocked into immobility. Her nose told her where she was. She turned. Staring back at her was Old Charger. The tunnel had opened up in a corner of Old Charger's stall. She would have to cross along one side of the stall in order to reach that gate. Old Charger had seemed threatening enough when she had looked at him through the fence, but here at knee level he reminded Abby of a volcano about to erupt.

"Now Abby, don't panic. Just stay calm. Slowly climb out. Good Charger, good boy. I'm just leaving. Got to cover this place up again. Good boy." Abby chattered away, saying whatever came into her mind. This was like a bad dream, and her movements were slow and awkward. Her mind was frozen, and her voice sounded raspy to her ears, but at least Old Charger wasn't doing anything.

She kept her eyes on Old Charger as she eased along the wall. The rough cement of the wall snagged at her fingers. She knew that she had reached the gate when she felt a sharp splinter slice her palm.

"Nice boy, easy now. Easy, easy." Abby tried to sound calm and talked to Old Charger the way Marcus did. "Somehow, old fellow, I don't think I'm convincing you." Her voice sounded rough and scared even to her.

"Here we are at the gate. Just lift the latch as I slide out. What's the matter with this stupid latch? It won't open!"

By now, Old Charger was snorting and stamping. Abby gave up any further attempts to get the latch open. Using the sides of the stall as a ladder, she scrambled over and landed in a twisted heap on the straw covered floor. Old Charger let out a bellow, and Abby ran.

It took a lot of scrubbing to clean all the mud and filth from her shoes. Even after she washed her hair, showered and changed her clothes, she could still smell Old Charger.

By the time everyone returned, Abby was settled on the bench that circles the big tree, reading.

Molly flopped down beside her. "Will I *ever* be glad when this play is over. I'm beginning to feel like a little slave girl, and I don't like it. What's that smell?"

Her question caught Abby off guard. Stalling for time, Abby asked, "What smell?"

"You got perfume on? It smells pretty good."

Abby relaxed against the tree, overwhelmed with relief. "Yeah. Mom sent it to me."

CHAPTER NINE

Different Families

After the futile adventure in tunnel exploration, Abby was content to let go of the search for the hidden room for a while. Instead, she helped Molly learn her lines for "Dangerous Journey" by giving her the cues. They rummaged through the attic for old clothes that would be useful in the play. One morning Abby brushed the dust from an old rocking chair and sat carefully as though she expected it to break under her. When it didn't, she proceeded to rock slowly, as she watched Molly sort old shoes.

"You know, Molly, you're OK."

"Girl, what are you talking about?" Molly paused in her work, looking at Abby with an impatient toss of her head.

"Girl" Abby's voice slid up in an imitation of Molly's. "I thought you would be just another dumb kid, and this would be the stupidest vacation ever. But, I was wrong. You're OK."

"Well thanks a whole heap." Molly continued sorting the shoes. "Don't try to imitate me, though. It doesn't sound right, somehow. There. That's all the shoes I can find that we can use. Let's get this stuff together."

They gathered up all the clothing and shoes and stuffed them into a big box. Then hurriedly, they returned the rest of the items to their original boxes.

"I suppose we should wash these, don't you?" Abby sneezed. "If anyone wears this stuff like this, your whole play will be nothing but a lot of sneezing."

The rest of the afternoon was spent washing, drying and carefully ironing the articles of clothing they had chosen. Some pieces were surprisingly colorful when they were clean. The girls felt quite proud of their handiwork.

"I'm sure glad I don't have to do this every day. This is a hot job." Abby unplugged the iron and set it aside to cool. The neatly folded stacks of shirts and dresses were carefully placed in a box, and newspapers were folded across the top.

"I was wrong, too." Molly's dimple flashed as she brushed vigorously at the shoes.

"About what?"

"You. I thought you were just another smart city kid who would come here and make fun of us. Then when you got here and made that dumb remark about us living in a play or something, I was sure. Marcus, too."

"Yeah, that was pretty stupid." Abby could feel her ears getting hot as she remembered that first ride to the Whitaker farm. "I was so surprised by all of you, I just couldn't think of anything to say."

"Surprised about us? Why? Didn't you know we were a mixed family?" Molly's eyes widened as Abby slowly shook her head. "Oh wow. That must have been quite a shock." The humor of the situation sank in, and the two girls began to giggle, then broke out in gusty laughter, rocking back and forth holding their sides.

The opening of "Dangerous Journey" was only a week away, and Abby was convinced it would never get off the ground. The twins practiced their parts constantly, giving each other the cues. After each rehearsal, discussion and disagreement over everything increased. Abby took refuge in Mr. Whitaker's study. It was quiet there, and she could read without having to listen to the twins argue.

One evening she was turning through a collection of pictures when Mr. Whitaker came into the room. He sat down at the big desk and began rummaging through the drawers.

"Ah. Here it is. I knew it was here someplace. Look at this, Abby." He held a picture out to her. "I've been thinking about what you said about choosing your family. Maybe this will help explain."

Abby felt her face get hot. She had hoped Mr. Whitaker had forgotten her remarks. It had been one of those dark rainy days when she felt so alone, and Molly had made some remark about Abby's moodiness. They got so involved in their argument, which turned to families, adopted parents, and stepparents. Abby had just yelled something like, "I don't see why grown-ups have to have their way always. Why don't they ask their kids before they split up or get married or whatever! And then they try to make us believe it's for *our* good." Then she had turned to see Mr. Whitaker standing behind her. He looked as though he was about to say something, but instead he turned and walked away. Abby wished she could just vanish. If only she could take back her angry words.

The whole scene came flashing back to her as she took the photo. It was a picture of Mrs. Whitaker sitting on a sofa with each arm around a small black child. The children were dressed in matching outfits of blue and white. "These are the twins, right?" Even as young as the twins were, Abby could see that Marcus was the serious one.

Mr. Whitaker nodded slowly. "We had been waiting for a long time for a family when we learned about these two children. They had been orphaned when a storm wiped out their little island village. The people from our church tried to find a black family to care for them, but they couldn't find anyone who would take both of them. We weren't sure we were up to handling two, but Norma and I just couldn't bear the thought of separating them. Besides," he smiled and spread his hands, "you can see that even at a very early age, Molly had those dimples."

Thoughtfully, Abby studied the photograph, then handed it back. "You know, Aunt Norma said that sometimes it's difficult for all of you, the twins being adopted and all. I wonder if it's that way for everyone." Abby watched Mr. Whitaker carefully, hoping he would say something to make her feel better about Al. After all, the more she thought about Al, the more she was convinced he must think of her as being in the way.

Mr. Whitaker leaned back, causing the chair to squeak under his weight. "I can't speak for anyone else, Abby, but I can say that I expected some problems when we adopted the twins. Especially in a small community like this one. There are some parts of the country where we wouldn't have been able to adopt them. But anytime you have parents and children, you will have problems. It's just part of life. The important thing is how you handle the problems."

"What kind of problems do you mean, Uncle Jake?"

Mr. Whitaker took a deep breath and spread his hands. "Some people don't take kindly to a white couple adopting black children. Some of them are rather rude to us."

"Well, I think you're a pretty cool family." Abby took a deep breath. "I wonder if Al thinks of me as a problem. I've been pretty rude to him and Mom." She looked at Mr. Whitaker. "I don't know how to make friends very well. I feel so *dumb*."

"Well, Abby, I have found that it usually works best if you just tell the other person how you feel, then give him a chance to think about it."

Abby sat silently, thinking about his words. Finally, she smiled and nodded. “Thanks. I’ll try it.” And with that, she left the room.

CHAPTER TEN

Abby's Debut

Abby was rudely awakened by Molly rushing about the room. She sat up, rubbing her eyes. "Why are you up at this hour of night? Is something wrong?"

Molly paused and gave Abby a look. "Don't hassle me, girl. I've got to get ready. This is **the day**, and I can't find my script."

"**The day**? What day? Oh, the play. But it isn't until tonight. Go back to bed." And Abby flopped back down and pulled the sheet up over her eyes.

Molly mumbled to herself and continued to search noisily for her copy of the play. Finally, she banged out of the room. Abby could hear her clattering down the stairs. A door slammed somewhere, then all was quiet.

Later, when Abby dressed and went downstairs, she found the house almost deserted. Mrs. Whitaker was in the kitchen making sandwiches. Abby snatched up a towel and tucked it into her belt like an apron. "Can I help?" She took a knife and began spreading mayonnaise across a slice of bread. After working steadily for what seemed a long time to Abby, Mrs. Whitaker poured a cup of coffee for herself and set a can of soda out for Abby. "Break time," she said, sitting down at the table.

“What are you planning to do with all these sandwiches? We must have hundreds here.” Abby gulped her soda, then coughed as it fizzed up the back of her throat.

“Well, everyone is going to be so busy today with the play that I thought we would just have sandwiches and quick things ready so each person can eat whenever it is best for him. Thanks for helping, Abby. It was beginning to look like a long job, having to do it by myself. I am surprised, though.” She paused to sip some coffee.

“Surprised? About what?”

“I was so sure Molly would talk you into a part in the play. She can be very persuasive when she puts her mind to it.” Mrs. Whitaker smiled at Abby.

Abby shook her head. “I know. She doesn’t give up easily. She really got on my nerves always harping about that play. But I just couldn’t be in it.”

“Why? Because of the twins?”

“The twins? No. Oh, you think that I don’t want to, that because they’re—” Abby stammered, then laughed. “Oh what a dumb thing to think! Excuse me, I don’t mean to be rude.” And she continued to laugh while Mrs. Whitaker watched her. “You know, I climbed up that hill back there, then slipped and rolled down it. I got caught in Old Chargers’ stall by accident, and I fell out of the hay loft. But no problem, I can handle it. I just *cannot* stand up in front of a crowd of people and do anything intelligent. I told Molly that. I thought you knew."

They returned to their work, and the stacks of sandwiches mounted. At last they stored the full trays in the refrigerator. After they set out stacks of paper plates, cups and everything else needed for supper, Mrs. Whitaker turned to Abby. "Thanks again. You have been a tremendous help. Maybe you should rest a little."

"I think I'll explore a little more." Abby smiled at her. "I won't have many more chances since I'll be leaving soon."

"Yes, I know. We'll miss you. Watch the time. You don't want to miss the opening curtain, and your mother will be here soon."

All morning as she had made sandwiches, Abby had been thinking about the cornhusk doll. She had asked Mrs. Whitaker, "If you wanted to hide something, where would you put it?"

Mrs. Whitaker had looked at her rather strangely and said, "Someplace where no one could find it, of course." After a pause, she then said something odd. "Sometimes the object you want to hide can be left out in plain view. If no one expects to find it, quite often it won't be seen."

Once again Abby packed her exploring gear in her backpack along with a couple of the sandwiches they had just made. She went to the tunnel entrance in the woods by a wide circular route. She wanted to say good-bye to the farm in her own way. After Mom and Al arrived, Abby wouldn't have time to visit her favorite places.

When she arrived at last at the entrance in the woods, Abby sat down and ate her sandwiches. It was so peaceful here with only the stirring of the leaves to interrupt the silence. Brushing the last of the crumbs from her fingers, she stood and taking her bag, slid down into the tunnel opening. This time Abby examined the tunnel entrance painstakingly for any niche or corner where something small might be tucked. "There's always a loose brick in a 'proper' mystery," she told herself, but there was only dirt here. After she had satisfied herself that there was not so much as a button hidden there, she entered the tunnel itself. Abby could almost hear the barking dogs and angry shouts of men behind her. She shoved aside the feeling of panic as she paused to shine her light slowly along the tunnel. "Now if I were five years old and had something to hide, where would I put it?" She resumed her examination, arriving finally at the hidden room. Setting her bag and light against the opposite wall, she pushed at the door. The door had swollen since they had last opened it. Abby pushed and tugged at the latch. "Nothing comes easy, I must say." The dirt wall absorbed her words like a dry sponge.

When Abby leaned all her weight against the door, it popped open, and she went sprawling into the darkness. It was a few minutes before she was able to sit up and look around. Her light was still in the passageway, casting a forlorn glow. She got to her feet and immediately fell back with a shriek. Pain streaked down her leg with each movement. She must have twisted it when she fell. It was the same leg she had hurt the time she fell off the bike. In addition to the throbbing in her leg, Abby felt a twist of real fear. "Is my leg broken?"

Cautiously, she pulled herself upright again, trying to keep as much weight off her injured leg as possible. Painfully, she hopped until she could retrieve her light and bag, then sat down just inside the door. Pain was pulsing through her leg, and it was all Abby could do to keep from crying. "I am really in a mess this time. How am I going to get back if I can't walk? Oh, this really *hurts*." The pain and frustration overwhelmed her, and she collapsed in sobs. Finally, worn out, she stopped, sniffed and mopped her face. Carefully, she moved her leg up and down. "This hurts like crazy, but nothing seems to be broken, after all. I guess I should keep moving if I'm ever to get out of here." Sniffling, she picked up the flashlight and resumed her survey of the room. Things looked different down here on the floor. "I wonder if those boards on the wall have always been there?" Abby limped over to the side nearest to her and shined her light along the beam. The board did not fit flat against the wall. There were little scooped out places as if some of the dirt wall had crumbled away. "If I were a little girl and didn't want anyone to take my only doll, what would I do? I would probably stick it behind something where I could reach. Of course!" As Abby began to examine the lower braces more carefully, her light flickered, then went out.

The dark closed in so intently that each time Abby blinked, she saw sparkles. Tentatively, she stretched out her arm until she located her bag. She felt around in the bag for the extra batteries, first carefully then frantically. With a flash of panic, she remembered. Marcus needed batteries for something, and she had given him hers. She just hadn't got around to replacing them. "This is just *great.*" As she kicked at the bag, the sudden motion wrenched her injured leg and brought tears to her eyes again. "I guess I'd better forget about that stupid doll and worry about getting out of here."

After several false starts, Abby discovered that by crawling on both hands and one knee, she could drag the injured leg without too much discomfort.

She moved carefully, trying to determine just where she was in the room. With a crash, she ran into the rickety table. "Ouch!" Abby paused to rub her shoulder. The table was about halfway so she could either go back, or go on around the room. "Shucks, I might just as well go on," Abby spoke softly, then repeated her words, yelling as loud as she could. No need to be quiet, no one could hear her.

By feeling the corner where the wall and floor meet, Abby felt her way around to the door. The floor was slippery with dust, and her movements churned up a continual cloud which threatened to choke her. Silence was roaring in her ears when she finally stopped to rest. By now the pain had settled down to a steady throb. She managed to get her good leg under her and pulled herself erect. As she clutched at the door frame for support, she felt a chunk of the support pull away from the wall, and she tumbled back onto the floor in a sobbing heap.

A worry began to nudge at the back of her mind, then grew until it crowded out the fear and pain. Abby had promised to help Molly dress and then stay backstage as prompter. It had amused Abby to think the very confident Molly was getting stage fright. "If you're so sure of yourself, why do you need me to sit back here?" she had nagged Molly. Molly had just looked at Abby, then resumed her work. She didn't even answer, and that made Abby even angrier. "I would really rather watch this play from the front with everyone else. Besides, Mom is coming, and I'd like to sit with her."

After another long look, Molly had picked up her things. At the doorway, she paused long enough to say, "Just forget it." Abby had followed Molly.

"Look," she said. "I'm sorry. I know this is important to you. I'll come help you."

Molly had looked so relieved that Abby realized just how important this play really was to Molly.

She groaned aloud now, here in the dark. "Now, Molly will think I changed my mind and won't help her after all."

Abby had no way of knowing how long she had been in the tunnel. She felt as though she had been hobbling and sliding along *forever*. In addition to the pain streaking down her leg, she felt a hot twist of desolation as she realized she wouldn't be there to help Molly as she had promised. Keeping her word was important to Abby. The pictures in her mind began to mock her, and she crunched over with a new pain. As she lay curled against the wall, frozen with fright and remorse, she felt a tug on her pants leg. Something slid across her ankle. This startled her out of her immobility. Chewing down the fear that was closing her throat, Abby jerked into motion. She snatched open her bag and began pawing over its contents. She spoke aloud as she identified each item. "Knife. Sweater. Apple." Crunching away on the apple, she continued. "Notebook. Pen. Batteries, dead as they are. Tissue. Wait a minute, I didn't have any tissue in here." She took out the wad of paper, then dropped it back into the bag. "I guess I'll have to look later."

The tunnel made an abrupt turn and just as she noticed a lessening of the darkness, she heard crying and voices. Slowly, her eyes adjusted. She had reached the small room beneath the stage. She couldn't understand what was being said. The words were overlaid with the sound of footsteps and heavy things being dragged about. Abby paused to rest. Before she tried to climb through the trapdoor, she just had to look into her bag. It was such a *relief* to be able to see again. She pulled out the wad of paper and held it to the dim light filtering down from above. Disappointment surged up the back of her throat. It was only a tight wad of dried leaves. Oh well, maybe she could still get up there in time to help Molly, and then she could take care of her leg.

Gritting her teeth against the pain, she dragged one of the boxes over so it was directly under the opening. After a great deal of pushing and pounding, she managed to shove the trapdoor open. It banged back against the floor with a dull crash, and Abby pulled herself through the opening, dragging her bag with her.

The brilliant glare of footlights blinded her, and she gasped and covered her eyes. She heard soft sounds all around her, then gradually, a clap here and there, growing until a great clatter of applause echoed. She felt herself being assisted to her feet and heard Molly say, "See Abby? I told you we'd find a place for you in our play."

"Yeah, Abby, nice of you to pop in." Marcus roared at his own joke.

Her stomach churned as she realized she had just barged into the middle of "Dangerous Journey." A sensation of extreme relief as well as searing pain in her leg overwhelmed her. She hopped over to a chair, collapsed onto it and did not remember anything else.

CHAPTER ELEVEN

The Discovery

The cornhusk doll was larger than Abby had imagined, and it stood beside her. Abby watched with fascination as its withered hand reached over and patted her cheek. She pulled back, but the doll persisted. It made a whispery sound when it moved.

"No. Get away from me." Abby shoved the hand away and watched as it shattered into tiny flakes that drifted away like snow. But something persisted, and Abby began to realize she was being shaken, gently at first, then more roughly.

"Abby? Abby! Wake up, dear. You're going to be all right. Oh, *do* wake up."

Abby pulled her eyes open. "Mom? I thought you were the doll."

Patricia hugged Abby. Just then the door banged open, and Molly poked her head around. "You know, Abby, it seems I'm always having to wake you up." Her dimples flashed. "As usual, it's lunch time, so hurry up." She banged the door again, and Abby could hear her clattering down the steps.

"Oh Mom, I have so much to tell you, I don't know where to begin." Abby hobbled to the bathroom. Her leg felt better as long as she didn't make any sudden turns.

Lunch was a noisy occasion. Molly and Marcus tossed jokes between them like a beanbag. Abby ate silently. She remembered the first lunch after she had arrived at the farm. Only now, these were her friends, and she felt at home. During a lull in the conversation, she looked at Mrs. Whitaker. "Aunt Norma, this is the same kind of soup we had the first day I was here. Did you realize that?"

Mrs. Whitaker looked at Abby's mother and laughed. "This girl has a memory that is unrelenting. You are right, Abby, and now, in honor of this special occasion, I have a special dessert. Come on guys, give me a hand." She motioned the twins to follow her, and the three of them disappeared into the kitchen. They returned with a huge tray of caramel apples all covered with nuts.

"Abby, I remember you said this is your favorite, right?"

Abby nodded and taking an apple by the stick, crunched into its tangy sweetness. "Um-perfect."

Later that afternoon, Abby carefully walked out to the tree bench. She leaned back and adjusted her leg so it was comfortable. It didn't really hurt anymore; it was just sore. Mr. Whitaker and her Mom had gone with her to the clinic in town earlier. The doctor had shaken his head and given her a scolding. "Kids. They're always falling in or off or out of something." He gave Abby a package of pills for the pain, a pink lollipop and made her feel like she was five years old.

"Mind if I join you, or is this just 'Private thoughts only'?" Abby jumped. Al had come up so quietly, she hadn't noticed him.

"Oh no. It's OK. Sit down." Abby patted the bench beside her.

"How's the leg? Does it hurt much?" The words were concerned but stiff. It occurred to Abby that Al wasn't all that concerned about her leg, he wanted to know how she felt about him. The sudden realization made her feel very grown-up and unexpectedly amused. She laughed.

"Did I say something funny?" He sounded puzzled.

"No, no. I just thought of something, that's all." Abby twisted around so she could look squarely at Al. "I was really mad at you, you know."

"Yes, I *do* know. Still mad at me?" His blue eyes twinkled at her.

"You did? Well, yes I guess I made it plain enough, didn't I?" Abby shook her head. "No, I'm not mad anymore. Actually, I think it will be good to get another point of view on things." She smiled at Al and leaned back against the rough bark of the tree. They sat in silence for a while, then Abby sighed. "You know, all the time I was stuck down in that dark tunnel, I knew I'd get out sooner or later. I had to, because nobody knew where I was. I was just afraid I wouldn't make it in time to help Molly with her lines if she needed me. When I finally did get out, it was such a relief. Then I conked out like that. I feel so embarrassed."

"No need to be. After all, you were the hit of the show." Al chuckled, then became serious. "Actually, everyone was very worried about you. Your mother and I arrived earlier than we expected, and they were all in a stew over where you were."

"I was afraid Molly would think I was really mad at her."

"Well, I don't know about that, but the show must go on, you know. At any rate, it was a tremendous relief for us all when you popped through the floor, looking like the dirt princess herself with your bag of tricks."

That brought a laugh to Abby's lips, and the two of them sat laughing at the picture Al had described.

"You'll be interested to know that Rob took that wad of paper you found and carefully straightened it all out."

"What was it?" Abby's curiosity twitched.

"It seems it was the remains of what must have been the cornhusk doll, but there was more."

"What? What?"

"A paper of some kind. He's having it analyzed. There was writing on it, but he needed some special equipment to examine it. He'll let you know what he finds."

Abby and Al talked for a long time. She then took Al on a short tour of the garden and introduced him to her favorite plants. Then he had to meet Old Charger.

As they made their way slowly back to the house, Abby broke the silence. "The Whitakers told me to call them Aunt Norma and Uncle Jake because it made them feel old to be called Mrs. or Mr. Whitaker all the time. And I kind of like to call them that, especially since I don't have any aunts or uncles. But it doesn't feel right to call you 'Dad,' and Mr. Cunningham seems weird. What should I call you?" She turned to look at him as she spoke.

"Well, Mr. Cunningham makes me think you're talking to my father, and you're right about 'Dad.' How about 'my friend Alan,' or 'Al' for short?"

"It's a deal, Al for short." Abby stuck out her right hand, and they solemnly shook hands.

The next morning was a busy one. Once again, Abby and her mother were packing Abby's things.

"It's a good thing we're not leaving until this afternoon." Abby's mother shook her head. "We'd never be ready." Abby kept interrupting by describing all the things she and the twins had done. "When we get back, I want to plant some things in that big planter out on the terrace."

They had just started eating lunch when Rob showed up. He pulled up a chair, waved aside Mrs. Whitaker's offer of lunch and carefully spread a square of rumpled paper in front of Abby.

"What's this?" It rattled as she picked it up, and a tiny piece broke away under her thumb.

"Careful." Rob pushed her hand holding the paper gently down to the table. "This, Abby, is what was inside the cornhusk doll."

Gingerly, Abby smoothed the brittle paper as much as she dared. "There's writing on it." She squinted at the faint brown lines. "It looks like 'something Madison ... I declare something, something Walker' ... it's a letter." She looked up at Rob. "Have you figured out what this is?" A flicker of excitement ran down her back.

"Yes. I took it to Dr. Arnold, who is head of the history department, and we have determined this is a Certificate of Manumission. Caleb Walker was evidently running north with a paper which declared him and his kin free. Either he didn't know what this paper contained, or no one would acknowledge it. It seems to be addressed to someone named Madison, but we couldn't make out the rest of the name."

Abby and Molly looked at each other and together said, "Poor little Sukey." Abby smoothed the edge of the paper. "Doesn't it make you wonder what happened to her? Did she stay around here, did she grow up, go to school, have children? Maybe she married a farmer."

Molly slapped the table. "Now Abby, just get that look out of your eyes. We are not, repeat *not* going on any more search parties."

Abby laughed, and everyone began talking about other things. Later though, she asked Rob something which had been on her mind for some time. "Rob, how did you know about the cornhusk doll and the treasure? There wasn't much said about it in the stuff we found at the library."

"Well," Rob cleared his throat and turned red. "I really didn't know anything about it. I just made it up."

"You made it up?" Abby's voice slid up the scale in disbelief. "Made it up? Listen to this, guys. He just made it up." Marcus and Molly stopped talking, and all three pairs of eyes were centered on Rob.

"Yeah. Look at it this way." Rob took a deep breath. "You, Abby, had such a chip on your shoulder about not needing anyone, that you couldn't walk without leaning to one side. Molly was working overtime being the sweet cheerful sunshine kid. Something needed to be done to make the two of you see each other as a real person. So I mentioned the treasure." He laughed a little. "Imagine my surprise when you went hunting at the library and came up with an account that mentioned a cornhusk doll. Then to top everything off, you actually found it." He shook his head.

Marcus began to chuckle, then the chuckle grew to a hearty guffaw. Molly and Abby joined in, and soon the four of them were gasping and holding their sides.

Marcus slapped Rob across the shoulders as they both roared. "Well, old man, you better be careful what you say. It's likely to backfire."

When they settled down a bit, Abby handed the brittle paper back to Rob. "What are you going to do with this?"

"I'm taking it to the director of the Lincoln Museum. They are interested in displaying it." Rob carefully slipped the paper into a protective cover.

In the rush of getting everything packed, the time slid by like butter on hotcakes. Much to Abby's surprise, the crowd at the train station included all the young people from their group meetings. She had an opportunity, finally, to introduce her mother and Al to these other friends. When the call came to board the train, Abby turned to the twins. Placing an arm around each, she gave a great hug. "Thanks for a great time. Remember now, next year you're coming to visit me. I want to show you *my* backyard."

The End